The adventures of otto

See Pip Flap

David Milgrim

Ready-to-Read

Simon Spotlight

New York London Toronto Sydney New Delhi

For Kendra

SIMON SPOTLIGHT
An imprint of Simon & Schuster Children's Publishing Division
1230 Avenue of the Americas, New York, New York 10020
This Simon Spotlight edition August 2018
Copyright © 2018 by David Milgrim
All rights reserved, including the right of reproduction in whole or in part in any form.
SIMON SPOTLIGHT, READY-TO-READ, and colophon are registered trademarks
of Simon & Schuster, Inc.
For information about special discounts for bulk purchases, please contact
Simon & Schuster Special Sales at 1-866-506-1949
or business@simonandschuster.com.
Manufactured in the United States of America 0219 LAK
2 4 6 8 10 9 7 5 3
Library of Congress Cataloging-in-Publication Data
Names: Milgrim, David, author.
Title: See Pip flap / David Milgrim.
Description: Simon Spotlight edition. | New York : Simon Spotlight, 2018. | Series: The
adventures of Otto | Series: Ready-to-read | Summary: With help from his friend Otto the
robot, Pip the mouse tries to fly. Identifiers: LCCN 2017050718 | ISBN 9781534416369 (hc) |
ISBN 9781534416352 (pbk) | ISBN 9781534416376 (eBook)
Subjects: | CYAC: Robots—Fiction. | Mice—Fiction. | Flight—Fiction.
Classification: LCC PZ7.M5955 Sdm 2018 | DDC [E]—dc23
LC record available at https://lccn.loc.gov/2017050718

See Tweet flap.

See Tweet fly.

Fly, Tweet, fly.

Bye, Tweet, bye.

See Pip flap.

Flap, flap, flap.

Flap, flap, flap, flap.

Flap, flap, flap,
flap, flap, flap,
flap, flap, flap,
flap, flap, flap,
flap, flap, flap.

See Pip flap
but not fly.

Look!

Look what Otto made!

See Pip fly!

Fly, Pip, fly!

Ho hum.

See Pip flap.

Flap, flap, flap.

Flap, flap . . .

. . . flop.

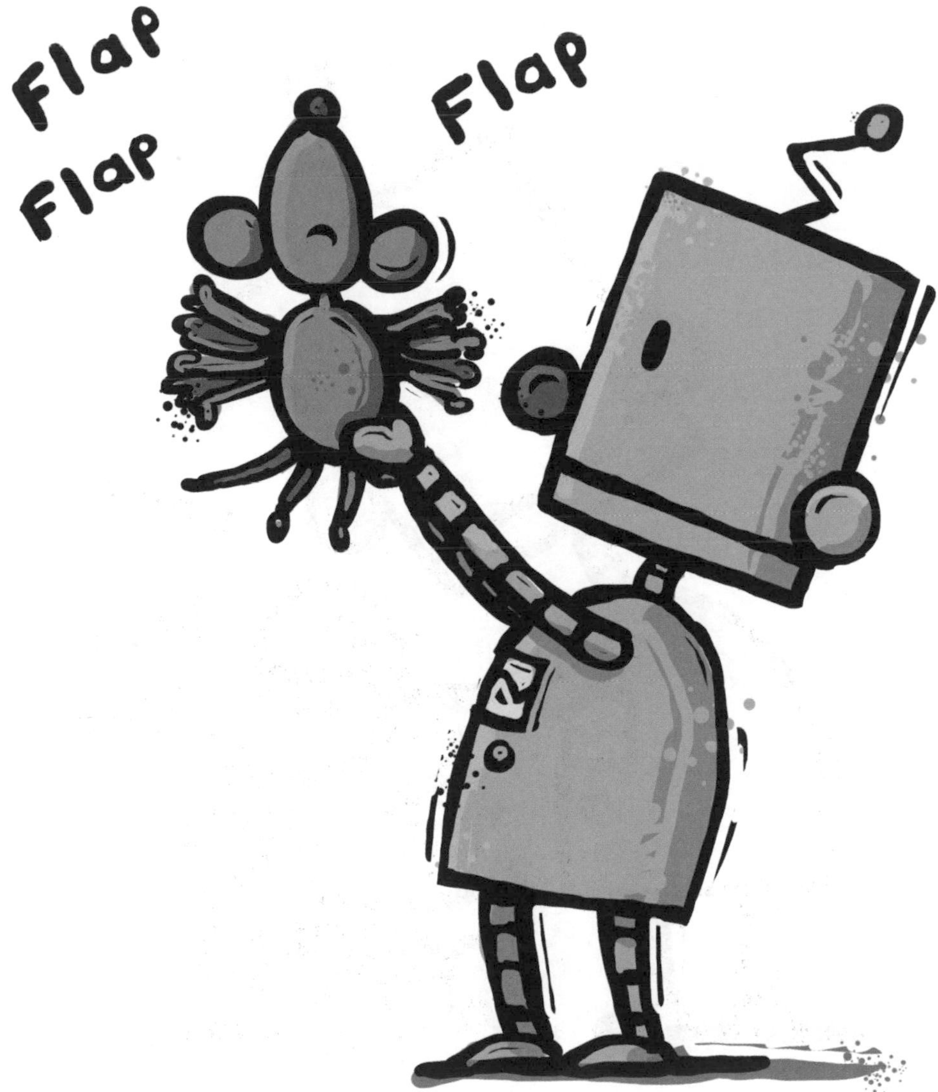
Flap
Flap
Flap

See Pip flap.

See Pip fly!

Fly, Pip, fly!